MISTER SCRATCH

Titles in Teen Reads:

Copy Cat TOMMY DONBAVAND	**Fair Game** ALAN DURANT	**Mama Barkfingers** CAVAN SCOTT
Dead Scared TOMMY DONBAVAND	**Jigsaw Lady** TONY LEE	**Pest Control** CAVAN SCOTT
Just Bite TOMMY DONBAVAND	**Mister Scratch** TONY LEE	**The Hunted** CAVAN SCOTT
Home TOMMY DONBAVAND	**Stalker** TONY LEE	**The Changeling** CAVAN SCOTT
Kidnap TOMMY DONBAVAND	**Dawn of the Daves** TIM COLLINS	**Nightmare** ANN EVANS
Ward 13 TOMMY DONBAVAND	**Joke Shop** TIM COLLINS	**Sitting Target** JOHN TOWNSEND
Deadly Mission MARK WRIGHT	**The Locals** TIM COLLINS	**Snow White, Black Heart** JACQUELINE RAYNER
Ghost Bell MARK WRIGHT	**Troll** TIM COLLINS	**The Wishing Doll** BEVERLY SANFORD
The Corridor MARK WRIGHT	**Insectoids** ROGER HURN	**Underworld** SIMON CHESHIRE
Death Road JON MAYHEW	**Billy Button** CAVAN SCOTT	**World Without Words** JONNY ZUCKER

Badger Publishing Limited, Oldmedow Road, Hardwick Industrial Estate, King's Lynn PE30 4JJ
Telephone: 01438 791037

www.badgerlearning.co.uk

MISTER
SCRATCH

TONY LEE

Mister Scratch ISBN 978-1-78147-961-2

Text © Tony Lee 2014
Complete work © Badger Publishing Limited 2014

Publisher: Susan Ross
Senior Editor: Danny Pearson
Publishing Assistant: Claire Morgan
Copyeditor: Cheryl Lanyon
Designer: Bigtop Design Ltd

2 4 6 8 10 9 7 5 3 1

CHAPTER 1

Liam looked at his watch for the fifteenth time that hour and knew with a sickening lurch in his stomach that Katie wasn't turning up.

Ever since they'd first met, Liam had known that Katie was the girl. And by that he meant *the* girl, the only girl, the one that he wanted to spend the rest of his life with. They were perfect for each other; they loved the same things, they enjoyed hanging out with each other and, more importantly for Liam, Katie laughed at his jokes. Not many people 'got' Liam's sense of humour. But a single line, a raised eyebrow, in fact anything that Liam did while they were together was guaranteed to get a laugh from Katie. And when she smiled, it was as if the world lit up...

Although now it looked like Liam's world was falling apart.

It had started a couple of weeks ago. Liam had suggested that they go to see the new superhero movie on at the Plaza, and Katie had cancelled at the last moment, claiming that she wasn't feeling too well. Liam took his best mate Darryl instead, calling her after the film to make sure she was OK. She seemed 'off', but Liam assumed that this was because of whatever was making her feel poorly.

It was a couple of days later when he saw a photo on Hayley Everett's Instagram, a photo that showed Katie and Hayley together in the Rock and Bowl the night that she had claimed she was ill. When Liam asked her about this, Katie became defensive, saying that Liam *shouldn't be checking up on everything she did*. They didn't talk for three days. And when they finally made up, Liam knew that something was broken in the relationship.

Liam started to worry about what Katie thought of him. Was she getting bored of him? Was she already bored of him? Had they been together the last couple of weeks purely because she didn't know the best way to dump him?

Feeling queasy, Liam pulled his mobile phone out of his backpack, checking it again for any missed messages. It was as empty as it had been three minutes earlier. Putting it away, Liam placed the bag back at his feet as he sat back on the bench, looking up at the sky as he let out the breath that he hadn't realised he'd been holding. Looking back at the world around him, he smiled at a small child walking past with her father, her free hand holding the largest candyfloss that Liam had ever seen. For a Thursday evening, Marley's Funfair was doing amazing trade. The only person who didn't seem to be having any fun was Liam. He checked his watch again. Twenty minutes late. Maybe Katie didn't like funfairs.

"She stood you up." The voice beside Liam spoke matter-of-factly, as if Katie standing Liam up was a statement, not a question. Turning to face the speaker, Liam was surprised at what he saw.

A middle-aged man sat beside Liam on the bench, as if he'd appeared out of nowhere. He wore a finely-made, charcoal-grey pinstripe suit with a white shirt and deep purple tie. His shoes were black and shiny, and upon one of them the man rested the silver tip of a black walking cane. The other end, shaped like a silver goat's head, rested in his right hand as his left stroked at his jet-black goatee beard. His hair was equally black, slicked back, his eyes red-rimmed, deep-blue and twinkling as he stared at Liam.

"I'm sorry, I was watching you check your watch and your phone. And you've been here for almost half an hour," he said. Liam shook his head.

"She's just late," he replied nervously, wondering to himself how this stranger had got so close without him realising. "She'll be here soon."

"Of course she will," the man said, looking across at the funfair. "Let's hope it's before the funfair closes." He smiled again, offering Liam his hand.

"I'm Mister Scratch, by the way," he said. "This is my funfair."

"I thought it was Marley's funfair?" Liam pointed at one of the signs. Mister Scratch nodded.

"It was. He owed me a debt. I took the fair," he said, twirling the cane around in his hand. "Anyway, I've told you my name..."

"I was told never to give my name to strangers," Liam replied. This made the strange man grin even more widely.

"Ah, but we're not strangers, are we?" he said. "I mean, I've told you my name and you're sitting in the middle of my funfair so, technically, you're in my house." He waved his cane around, indicating the Waltzers, the Dodgems and the Amusement Arcade before looking back at Liam.

"So it's actually incredibly rude of you not to tell me your name now, *Liam*, isn't it?"

Liam stared at the man in shock, half rising from his seat as he did so.

"How do you know my name?" he asked, the anger rising in his voice. "Have you been stalking me? Are you one of *those*?"

Calmly, Mister Scratch tapped the side of Liam's backpack. There, drawn in marker, was a graffiti-style LIAM.

"People don't usually walk around with someone else's name on their bag," he said, the constant smile on his face now starting to irritate Liam, who sat back down feeling foolish.

"Sorry," he said as he held his hand out. "I'm Liam, but you already know that."

Mister Scratch took the hand and shook it solemnly.

"A pleasure to meet you, Liam," he said. "Now why don't you tell me about the girl that's stood you up, and we'll see if we can do something about it."

In the weeks that followed, Liam couldn't explain what had made him talk to Mister Scratch that evening. All he remembered was that, as he looked into Mister Scratch's eyes, he knew without a doubt that by telling Mister Scratch his problems everything would be all right.

It wasn't until later that same night that he would realise just how wrong he was.

CHAPTER 2

As Liam told Mister Scratch about Katie
and his concerns that she was getting bored with
him, the older man sat completely still, almost
statue-like, as he listened. Liam didn't mean to
talk for so long, but once he started he found that
it was actually rather nice to explain his worries
and concerns about his relationship to this
complete stranger. He talked about the first time
he met Katie, the first time that he knew that she
was the girl he wanted to go out with, and the
first time that he was able to muster the courage
to speak to her. He talked about how Darryl
had mocked him, saying that she was 'out of his
league', and how it had felt so good to push that

back in Darryl's face when Katie agreed to go to the cinema with him. He didn't think that Darryl liked Katie that much, probably scared that she would take Liam away from him, that he would lose his best mate – and no matter what Liam said, no matter how much he tried to reassure Darryl, he knew that his words were falling on deaf ears.

"Tell me why she's not here," Mister Scratch interrupted. "Tell me your fears."

Liam paused, considering the question. It was one he'd been asking himself for the last half hour.

"She's been distant lately," he admitted. "She's been harder to talk to, as if she's had a secret that she's keeping from me."

"Does she keep secrets?" Mister Scratch stared at Liam, his eyes unwavering. In the end Liam had to look away.

"No," he replied. "That is, not that I know of. I mean, who knows, eh?"

"You're her boyfriend," Mister Scratch answered. "You should know."

Liam nodded. "I know," he admitted. "But I don't. All I know is that a couple of weeks ago she went out with Hayley and she told me she was ill."

"Maybe she felt sorry for Hayley? Maybe Hayley made her go and she felt bad for you?" Mister Scratch shifted position on the bench, watching two dogs playing with each other across the park. Liam shook his head.

"No, she would have told me the truth. If I hadn't seen the pictures on Instagram, I'd never have been the wiser."

"And so you confronted her." Again, it was said as a statement rather than as a question. Liam nodded.

"I was angry. It seemed the right thing to do."

Mister Scratch nodded. "You did what you thought was right. That's admirable. And she resented you for it."

"Hold on, 'resented' is a bit harsh," Liam said, feeling uneasy. "She was angry with me for a bit – "

"She hasn't turned up today," Mister Scratch interrupted, his voice suddenly dark and commanding. "She hasn't turned up today because she hates you. She thinks you're a joke."

"That's not funny," Liam snapped, standing up. "You don't say something like that to a complete stranger – "

"*Sit down.*" The two words were spoken with such command that Liam found himself sitting immediately back onto the bench, like a dog learning a trick. Mister Scratch sat back, staring long and hard at the boy beside him.

"Do you want to know where she is right now?"

he asked. "I mean, truly and deeply, you want to know where she is right now, even if it's an answer that you don't want to hear?"

"You don't know," Liam said, the uneasy feeling rising from his stomach and now tap-dancing up his spine. "All you know is what I've said."

"Katie Williams. Hayley Everett. Darryl Carr. Three surnames you haven't told me, Liam. Three names I've known since the day they forced their way out of their mothers, mewling for the first time, slapped by the doctor to bring them to life. I was there for every birth," Mister Scratch said, the words slow and meaningful. "I was there for your birth, Liam Lewis."

Liam didn't like this game now. Someone was playing a serious wind-up on him, and it wasn't funny any more. But somewhere deep inside his soul he knew that Mister Scratch wasn't playing around, that somehow he did know these names, and that somehow he *did* know what Katie was doing right now. He looked around anxiously, hoping more than anything in the world to see her walking towards him, late because of a broken-down bus. Oh, how they'd laugh when she told him the story. He could almost see it.

Almost.

Liam *didn't* want to know. He didn't want to speak to this strange man any more. He wanted to get up from the bench and run away, far away from this man, his weird cane and his creepy funfair. But he didn't.

"Tell me," he said.

CHAPTER 3

Mister Scratch thought for a moment, looking away from Liam to smile at an old woman walking past, a three-year-old girl in her arms. Liam assumed that the girl was the lady's granddaughter, but now he wasn't sure of anything.

"Katie won't be here today," Mister Scratch spoke, the sudden words making Liam jump as he returned his attention to the well-dressed man with the walking cane.

"Why?" he found himself asking. Mister Scratch looked at him and smiled although there was no warmth in the expression.

"Because she's at the cinema with Darryl Carr," he replied matter-of-factly. "She's gone to see that superhero movie that you wanted her to see a couple of weeks back."

"That's rubbish," Liam replied. "She didn't want to go to see it. She wouldn't go with Darryl to watch a movie she wasn't interested in."

"Who said they were watching the movie?" Mister Scratch raised an eyebrow. "No, they've found two seats in the back row. The last thing on their minds is the film. After all, Katie isn't that bothered about it, and Darryl's seen it before. With you, in fact."

"No." Liam shook his head. "I don't believe it. Darryl wouldn't do that to me."

"Darryl's wanted Katie since the moment they met," Mister Scratch continued. "He's only stayed best mates with you because it gave him a chance to spend time with her. And now you're falling apart, relationship-wise, he's sneaked in like a vulture, flying Katie away from you and into his arms." He leaned forwards, closer now to Liam.

"He's a very good kisser," he whispered. "Katie keeps telling him so."

"Lies," Liam whispered. "You don't know what Katie's saying right now. This is all some kind of sick joke to you."

"Yes, you're probably right." Mister Scratch rummaged around in his jacket pocket as he spoke. "I mean, I'd have to have some serious supernatural powers to be able to hear what she was saying right now, as she nuzzles her face into Darryl's ear, as she kisses his neck." He pulled out a pack of cigarettes with a triumphant smile. Opening them up, he offered one to Liam.

"Smoke?"

Liam shook his head. Shrugging, Mister Scratch took one out of the pack, placing it in his mouth. As he put the crumpled pack away with his left hand, he held up his right hand, lighting the cigarette.

"Yes sir, I'd need some serious superpowers indeed," he muttered to himself as the flame lit the end of the cigarette. Liam found himself doing a double-take.

Mister Scratch wasn't holding a lighter.

The flame was coming from the tip of Mister Scratch's index finger, as if it was a candle. The cigarette was lighting from it, and there was no artificial way that Mister Scratch could have set this up. Seeing Liam's expression, Mister Scratch grinned. The flame at the end of his finger winked out of existence.

"Good trick, isn't it?" he asked, watching Liam carefully as he spoke. "She's laughing about you, Liam. Right now she's laughing, telling Darryl that you were nothing more than a sympathy boyfriend, and that once she'd agreed to go out with you she couldn't get out of it. Have you ever had one of those days where you go with your parents to a relative that you don't like, and you have to spend the whole day being nice to them, hoping that very soon your parents will get the hint and you'll be able to leave? That's Katie."

"No."

"Oh, in case you didn't get it, the relative that she doesn't want to hang around with? That's you. Not literally, but you get the idea."

Liam could feel tears welling at the back of his eyes. Even though he hadn't seen Katie cheating on him, Mister Scratch's words brought up images almost as real as if he could see it unfolding in front of him. Katie and Darryl kissing in the back row. Holding hands. Katie telling Darryl that Liam was a joke. Darryl agreeing.

It was all so real.

"It doesn't have to be this way though," Mister Scratch spoke again, jerking Liam out of the dream.

"What do you mean?" Liam asked. "I've lost her. What else can I do?"

"Answer one question," Mister Scratch said, once more focused on the cane as he spun it in his fingers. "What if you could make a deal, one that would make her true to you?"

Liam didn't understand what Mister Scratch was saying. "You mean like three wishes? Like a genie?"

"Very similar, but it's just one wish. More a desire, really," Mister Scratch replied, his eyes now boring into Liam's own as they looked at each other. "All you have to do is wish, here and now, that wherever she is right now, she'll come back to you and love you forever."

Liam stared at Mister Scratch in dumb shock.

"Go on. Say it."

Liam stood up.

"For what?" he asked. "I mean, why would you give me this for nothing? What do you want?"

Mister Scratch shrugged. "I do it for true love," he replied. "Something I never experienced."

Liam looked across the park at the couples laughing, the people enjoying each other's company, and for one small, broken moment he wished more than anything that he could have that with Katie. His mind made up, he looked down at Mister Scratch.

"I wish that wherever she is right now, she'll come back to me and love me forever," he said, already regretting the choice the moment he spoke the words.

But by then it was too late. And in the years that followed, Liam would always return to this point of the story in his mind, knowing that this was the moment that everything went wrong.

CHAPTER 4

Nothing happened.

Liam looked around, confused. "So where is she?" he asked. "You said if I wished it, it'd come true."

Mister Scratch rose to face Liam. "It takes time," he said. "Go home and she'll find you there, I'm sure."

Liam nodded, somehow knowing that Mister Scratch wasn't lying. Without even looking back at the strange man in the pinstripe suit, Liam left the park at a run, getting as far away as he could from the funfair as quickly as possible.

It was on Radcliffe Road that he saw the ambulance and the police cars.

Stopping beside the small crowd that had gathered to see whatever was happening, Liam tried to peer through them to see what was going on. All he could see was a car, a white, sporty type, which had smashed into a tree at speed, judging by the impact damage to the front bumper. The windscreen was smashed and there were red marks that looked like smeared blood on the bonnet.

"What happened?" he asked. A woman no older than his mother looked around to face him.

"Idiot was drunk and speeding along Radcliffe Road while texting," she said. "Hit a kid, crashed into the tree."

"What kid? Are they in the ambulance?" Liam tried to get a better look, a morbid curiosity taking hold now. *Was it someone from his school? Was it someone he might know?*

The woman shook her head. "If she is in the ambulance, she's not going to get better. The policeman over there said to his mate that she was dead on impact. Stupid girl, running across the road without looking."

Liam stepped back with a sickening feeling in his stomach. "How long ago did this happen?" he asked. The woman looked at her watch.

"Oh, about thirty minutes back."

Liam thought he was going to throw up, turning quickly from the crowd and walking away, pulling the phone out of his backpack. Thirty minutes ago was while he was waiting for Katie, and if...

No. He couldn't believe that the dead girl in the ambulance was his Katie. Mister Scratch had told him otherwise. But then, how did he know anything? Magicians did tricks like the one Mister Scratch had done every day. Opening his contacts list, he found the contact named KATIE and pressed 'connect'. Earlier on it had gone straight to voicemail, but this time it clicked through, ringing.

Behind him, on the ground beside the ambulance, a phone in a blood-spattered handbag started to ring.

Liam switched the call off, backing away in horror as he clicked another contact, KATIE HOME. After two rings it was answered by the voice of Katie's mother.

"H-hello?"

"Mrs Williams? It's Liam..."

The voice at the end of the phone started to sob. "Oh Liam! Have you heard? I was going to call, but things... I'm about to go to the hospital, the police are here."

"Katie?"

"She's..." Mrs Williams paused as she started to cry. "She was hit by a drunk driver. She died instantly. She was running to meet up with you, she knew she was late."

Liam felt sick. Mister Scratch had lied. And more importantly, as Katie had lain dying, Liam had been sitting in a park no more than a three-minute walk away, complaining about her to a complete stranger.

"I'm so sorry," he said, but the phone was already dead. In a stunned silence, Liam put the phone carefully away and walked home.

His parents were out when he arrived, so he was alone when he crumpled to the floor and started to cry, deep racking sobs that were pulled out from his very soul.

Katie was dead.

He couldn't believe it, couldn't accept it. It wasn't true, just like everything Mister Scratch had said wasn't true. She hadn't been with Darryl. She hadn't been looking to leave him. She had been running to meet Liam and she still loved him.

"I love you, Katie," he whispered to himself. "I'll love you forever."

There was an aluminium baseball bat in the umbrella stand beside the door, and for a moment Liam considered taking it and swinging, smashing anything he could find, screaming the pain and anger out of his body as he did so... but he knew that, in the end, nothing was going to stop this hurt. If only...

The doorbell stopped his self-pity for a moment. It rang. And then it rang again. A chill ran down Liam's spine as he remembered Mister Scratch's words.

All you have to do is wish, here and now, that wherever she is right now, she'll come back to you and love you forever.

Getting up, Liam walked to the door and opened it. He guessed it was most likely a neighbour offering their condolences, or the police wanting a statement. He wasn't expecting what he saw.

Her neck at an impossible angle, her arm visibly broken, her face and body awash in blood, Katie was in the front-door porch, lurching towards him.

CHAPTER 5

Liam went through a series of emotions in the space of a second. The first was joy at Katie's appearance. She wasn't dead and everything was going to be fine. The second, as she spoke, was one of utter terror.

"Luv.... yooo...."

Her unbroken arm rose up as she staggered towards him like an extra in a zombie movie. Her eyes were glazed and unseeing, a small piece of bone jutted out of her shoulder. Liam staggered back from the door as she fell against it, lurching forwards still. Once more Mister Scratch's deal echoed in Liam's ears.

All you have to do is wish, here and now, that wherever she is right now, she'll come back to you and love you forever.

She'd been dead in the ambulance when he'd made the wish. Her own mother had confirmed this. Somehow, Mister Scratch's deal had come true. Katie had come back from the dead to find Liam. She loved him forever.

Liam hadn't realised that the baseball bat was now in his hand, taken from the umbrella stand as he fell backwards. As Katie, moaning and stumbling towards him, dripped blood onto the carpet, Liam realised that this wasn't his Katie. His Katie was dead. This was just the body, a shell – and if he let her touch him, who knew what she'd do? Was she a zombie? How could he leave her like this?

In the days that followed, when the police asked him what went through his mind at this point, he was never able to answer. He didn't think that anything actually went through his mind, he honestly believed that, at that moment, when he faced zombie Katie lurching through his door, reality gave way to a different state of mind and instinct took over.

He didn't remember hefting the baseball bat or swinging it at her head as he screamed. He didn't remember it hitting her head, but he remembered the sound, the sucking, crunching noise that it made as the aluminium bat hit human skull. It was a sound that he'd remember for the rest of his life.

Zombie Katie fell to the floor, her now unseeing eyes staring blankly at Liam as he leaned against the wall, the bloodied baseball bat tumbling from his fingers as he stared down at the body. Liam took deep breaths, trying to calm himself. He'd almost managed it when the phone rang.

Picking it up, he couldn't take his eyes off Katie's dead body as he spoke.

"Hello?"

"Liam? Is that you?" It was Mrs Williams. "Is Katie with you?"

"What do you mean?" Liam looked slowly down at the phone as if it was some kind of snake. "Katie's dead!"

"She's what?" The voice was distraught.

"You said on the phone, when I called you..." Liam's voice trailed off as he picked up the mobile phone from his backpack, checking his recent calls.

There was no outgoing call made that day to Katie's landline. There was no way that he could have spoken to Katie's mother.

"When you called me?"

Liam's legs gave way and he slumped to the floor. "I don't understand," he whispered. "She was hit by a car..."

"She was, but apparently when she got to the hospital, she disappeared."

"Hospital?"

"Of course the hospital, Liam! She broke her shoulder bone and her wrist! What's wrong with you?"

Liam stared at the body in front of him.

"I was told she was dead," he said. "That she died instantly."

"Whoever said that was wrong." Mrs Williams's voice was anxious. "We need to find her before she hurts herself. The doctors said she was concussed, that all she kept saying was your name. And then she disappeared. We think she's on her way to you. She was late for your date and she felt really guilty."

Liam started to cry. "She was going to break up with me wasn't she?" he asked.

"Of course not! She loved you!"

"But what about Hayley?"

"Hayley? Oh, they'd planned everything out already."

"Planned everything out?"

"Your birthday party," Mrs Williams said. "It was going to be a surprise. Hayley helped her find a venue, the Rock and Bowl on the High Street."

The Rock and Bowl. Where Hayley had taken the Instagram.

"Katie was very worried that all the secretive behaviour might have made you think she didn't want to be with you, but you couldn't be more wrong."

Liam started to laugh. It wasn't a 'funny joke' kind of laugh, it was a dark, broken one as he dropped the phone to the floor. Katie hadn't been cheating on him; she'd been planning a party for him. She didn't want to dump him; she was worried he was going to dump her. And she hadn't died when the car hit her; she'd been badly injured and confused, looking for the one person who could look after her. Liam.

The boy who'd killed her with one swing of a baseball bat.

The laughter turned into tears now, the sobs becoming one long, heartfelt scream into the night as Liam, his mind rebelling at the enormity of what he had done to Katie, finally... broke.

And in a park, with a funfair reaching the end of its day, a man in a pinstripe suit checked his pocket watch for the time, looked up to the sky and smiled.

"Another satisfied customer," Mister Scratch said to himself as he rose from the bench and walked off, looking for another lost soul to take.

THE END